ISBN 0-439-23463-8

12 11 10 9 8 7 6 5 4 3 2   0 1 2 3 4 5/0

Printed in Belgium
First Scholastic printing, October 2000

MARCUS PFISTER
THE RAINBOW FISH

CHOLASTIC

MARCUS PFISTER
THE RAINBOW FISH

TRANSLATED BY J. ALISON JAMES

SCHOLASTIC INC.

New York Toronto London Auckland Sydney
Mexico City New Delhi Hong Kong

One day, a little blue fish followed after him. "Rainbow Fish," he called, "wait for me! Please give me one of your shiny scales. They are so wonderful, and you have so many."

What good were the dazzling, shimmering scales with no one to admire them? Now he was the loneliest fish in the entire ocean.

One day he poured out his troubles to the starfish. "I really am beautiful. Why doesn't anybody like me?"

"I can't answer *that* for you," said the starfish. "But if you go beyond the coral reef to a deep cave you will find the wise octopus. Maybe she can help you."

The Rainbow Fish found the cave. It was very dark inside and he couldn't see anything. Then suddenly two eyes caught him in their glare and the octopus emerged from the darkness.

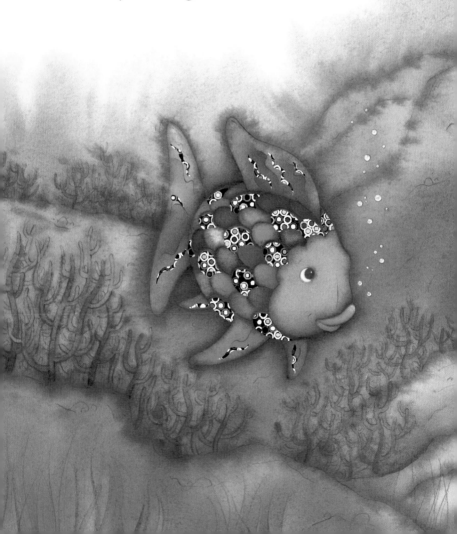

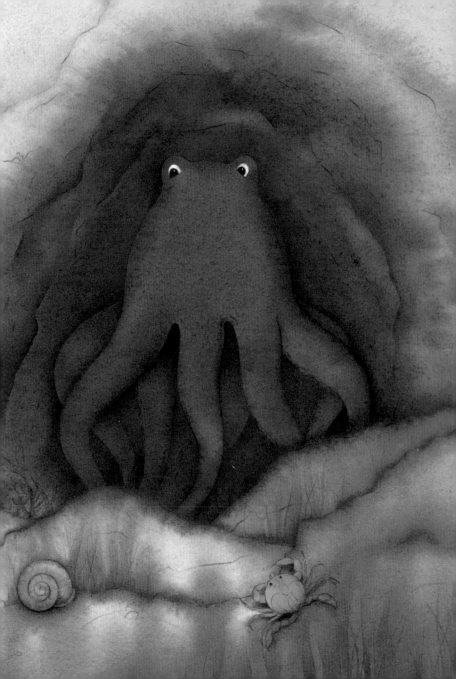

"I can't . . ." the Rainbow Fish started to say, but the octopus had already disappeared into a dark cloud of ink.

Give away my scales? My beautiful shining scales? Never. How could I ever be happy without them?

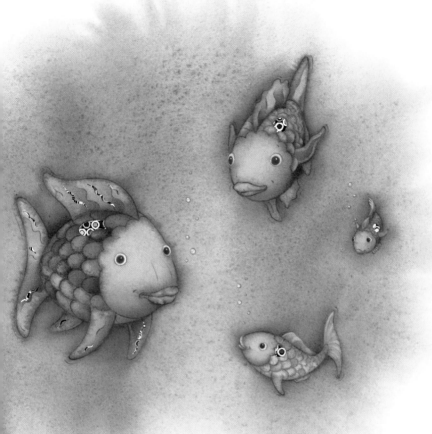

Finally the Rainbow Fish had only one shining
scale left. His most prized possessions had been
given away, yet he was very happy.

"Come on, Rainbow Fish," they called. "Come
and play with us!"

"Here I come," said the Rainbow Fish and,
happy as a splash, he swam off to join his friends.

This edition is only
available for distribution through
the school market.

SCHOLASTIC INC.

0-439-23463-8